This book belongs to:

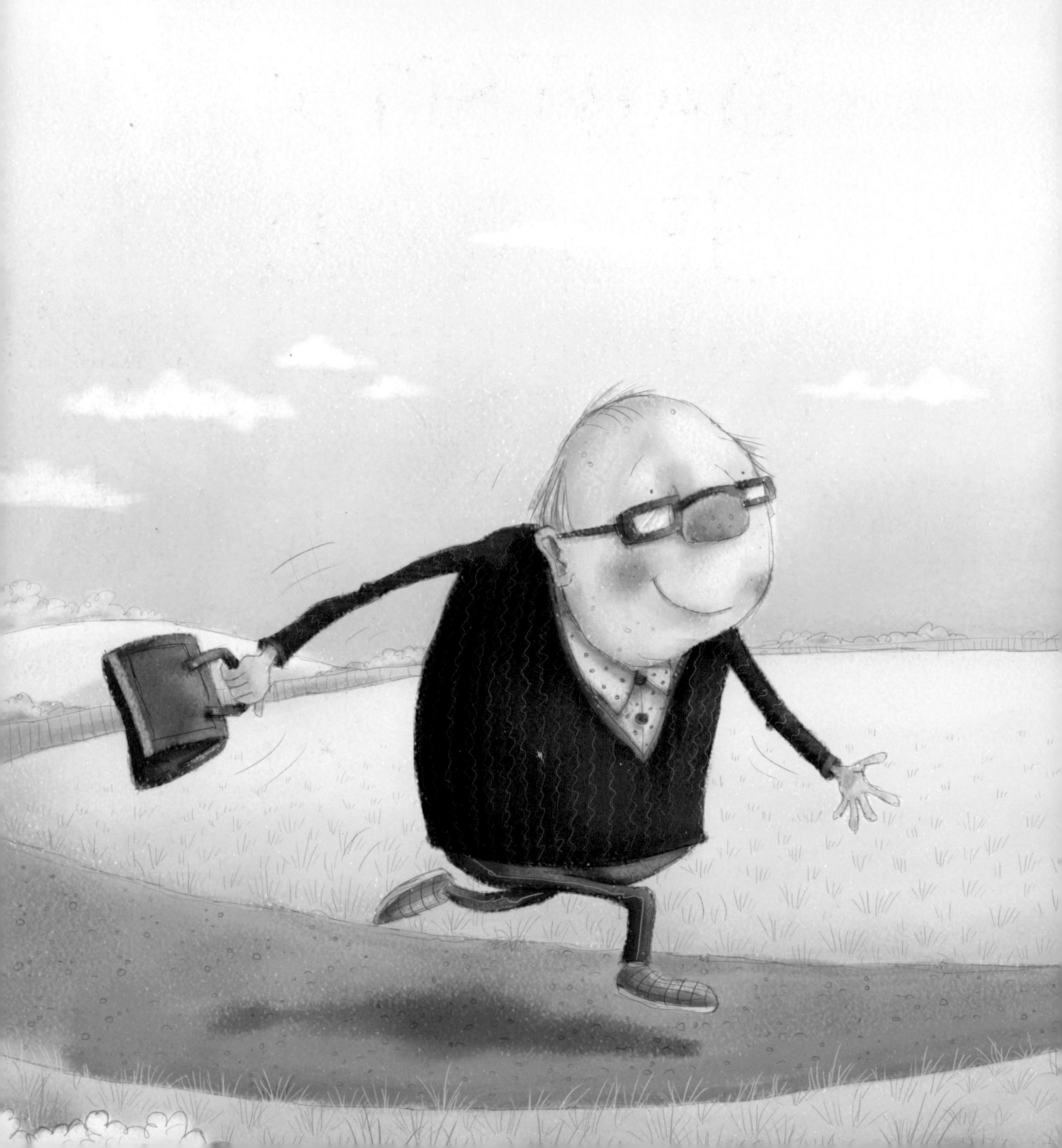

How to
Babysit a
Grandad

by Jean Reagan

illustrated by
Lee Wildish

A division of Hachette Children's Books

Babysitting a grandad is fun – if you know how.
When your grandad rings the doorbell, what should you do?

Hide!

You might wiggle and want to giggle.
But don't yell, "Grandad!" Not yet. Shhhhh . . .

HOW TO STAY QUIET:

*Pretend you're a shark
waiting for lunch.

*Act like a pirate spy.

*Be as still
as a lion statue.

As soon as your grandad says, "I give up,"
pop out and shout, **"HERE I AM!"**

When your mum and dad leave, pat your grandad's hand and say, "Don't worry. They always come back."
Then right away, ask him if he's hungry.

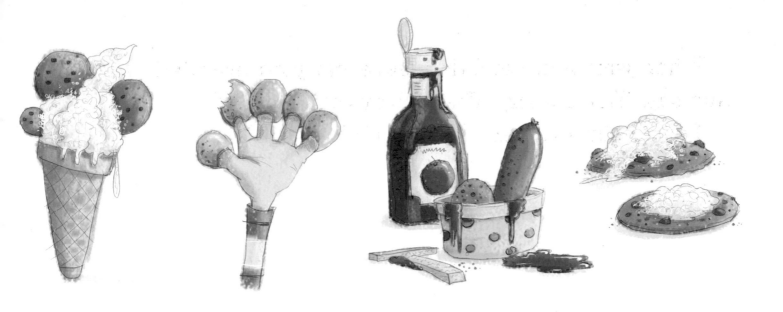

SNACKS FOR A GRANDAD:

- ⭐ Ice cream topped with cookies.
- ⭐ Olives served on fingertips.
- ⭐ Anything dipped in ketchup.
- ⭐ Cookies topped with ice cream.

After snacks, it's time to take your grandad for a walk.

When it's cold, bundle up.

When it's sunny, sunscreen up – especially the top of his head.

Remember to grab his hand when you cross the street, and remind him to look both ways.

WHAT TO DO ON A WALK:

* Step over pavement cracks.
* Look for lizards, cool rocks, and dandelion puffs.
* If there's a puddle or a sprinkler, show him what to do.

When you're back at home, have him shut his eyes while you get ready. And then . . .

HOW TO ENTERTAIN A GRANDAD:

* Somersault across the room.
* Put on a scary play.
* Show off your muscles.

You may want to have some extra tricks –
grandads always clap for more.

Pretty soon he'll want to join the fun, so play *with* your grandad, too.

HOW TO PLAY WITH A GRANDAD:

✳ March with your drum.
(Give him a kazoo.)

✳ Build a pirate cave.
(Make sure you can both fit.)

Watch out for sharks in the water!
(Don't let your feet touch the floor!)

When your grandad says, "Naptime," it's time for his nap. The best way to put him to sleep is to have him read a *looooooooooong* book,

over

    and

        over

           and

               over

                  and

                     . . . Z Z Z Z Z z z.

Even if you're sleepy, too, babysitters have to stay awake. While he naps, draw a picture for his fridge.

WHAT TO DRAW FOR A GRANDAD:

✳ A pirate-shark battle.

✳ Your favourite dinosaur.

✳ You and your grandad splashing in a puddle.

Then . . .

. . . wake up your grandad!

YOU MIGHT WANT TO TRY:

✶ Lifting him with your muscles.

✶ Tickling his nose and his toes.

✶Singing "Row, Row, Row Your Boat"
softly, then LOUDER and **LOUDER**.

Now ask, "Will Mum and Dad be home soon?"
Your grandad will look at the clock and say, "Yikes!
Soon! VERY soon!"

Good babysitters can't leave messes, so turn on some
bouncy music and get to work.

When you hear your mum and dad, grab your grandad's hand and pull him behind the couch. Show him how to be quiet (check How to Stay Quiet) and whisper, "See, Grandad. They always come back."

Now comes the hardest part: goodbye time.

HOW TO SAY GOODBYE TO A GRANDAD:

★ Surprise him with the picture.

★ Give him a hug and a kiss, a hug and a kiss, a hug and a kiss.

★ And ask, "When can I babysit you again?"

Purrrr Purrrr

For John and Jane
and their Grandpa John and Grandma Janice
—J.R.

For Roy Wildish & Dennis Gates,
you shall always be remembered.
—L.W.

First published in the United States by Alfred A. Knopf, an imprint of Random House
Children's Books, a division of Random House, Inc., New York.

This edition first published in the UK by Hodder Children's Books.

The right of Jean Reagan to be identified as the author and Lee Wildish as
the illustrator of this Work has been asserted by them in accordance with the
Copyright, Designs and Patents Act 1988. All rights reserved.

A catalogue record of this book is available from the British Library.

HB ISBN: 9781 444 91587 7
PB ISBN: 978 1 444 91588 4

Printed in China

10 9 8 7 6 5 4 3 2 1

Hodder Children's Books is a division of Hachette Children's Books,
338 Euston Road, London, NW1 3BH
An Hachette UK Company

www.hachette.co.uk

More fabulous Lee Wildish picture books:

9781 444 90015 6

Kes Gray and Lee Wildish

Leave Me Alone

Bears, Bears, Bears!

9781 444 90679 0

Illustrated by
Lee Wildish

Martin
Waddell

Kes Gray

MUM
AND
DAD
GLUE

Illustrated by
Lee Wildish

0 95711 340 9780

Jacob
O'Reilly
Wants a Pet

Lynne
Rickards and Lee Wildish

9780 340 988398 8

TOYS

FIRE